ALLOSAURUS

ANASTASIA SUEN

Rourke
Educational Media

A Division of
Carson
Dellosa
Education

rourkeeducationalmedia.com

SCHOOL to HOME
CONNECTIONS
BEFORE AND DURING READING ACTIVITIES

Before Reading: *Building Background Knowledge and Vocabulary*

Building background knowledge can help children process new information and build upon what they already know. Before reading a book, it is important to tap into what children already know about the topic. This will help them develop their vocabulary and increase their reading comprehension.

Questions and Activities to Build Background Knowledge:

1. Look at the front cover of the book and read the title. What do you think this book will be about?
2. What do you already know about this topic?
3. Take a book walk and skim the pages. Look at the table of contents, photographs, captions, and bold words. Did these text features give you any information or predictions about what you will read in this book?

Vocabulary: *Vocabulary Is Key to Reading Comprehension*

Use the following directions to prompt a conversation about each word.

- Read the vocabulary words.
- What comes to mind when you see each word?
- What do you think each word means?

Vocabulary Words:
- *apex*
- *asteroid*
- *carnivore*
- *dewclaw*
- *homestead*
- *Jurassic*
- *plesiosaurs*
- *pterosaurs*
- *quarry*
- *theropod*

During Reading: *Reading for Meaning and Understanding*

To achieve deep comprehension of a book, children are encouraged to use close reading strategies. During reading, it is important to have children stop and make connections. These connections result in deeper analysis and understanding of a book.

 ## Close Reading a Text

During reading, have children stop and talk about the following:

- Any confusing parts
- Any unknown words
- Text to text, text to self, text to world connections
- The main idea in each chapter or heading

Encourage children to use context clues to determine the meaning of any unknown words. These strategies will help children learn to analyze the text more thoroughly as they read.

When you are finished reading this book, turn to the next-to-last page for **Text-Dependent Questions** and an **Extension Activity**.

TABLE OF CONTENTS

CRUMBLING BONES

After the American Civil War ended in 1865, soldier Marshall P. Felch went home. The army didn't need him anymore. Felch went back to Massachusetts. Two years later he married Amanda. They moved to Colorado to start a farm.

A new **homestead** law allowed the family to claim 160 acres of land in the West. They just had to pay a small fee and live there for five years. Then the land would belong to them.

On that land, Felch saw fossils in the rocks. When he tried to pick them up, they crumbled.

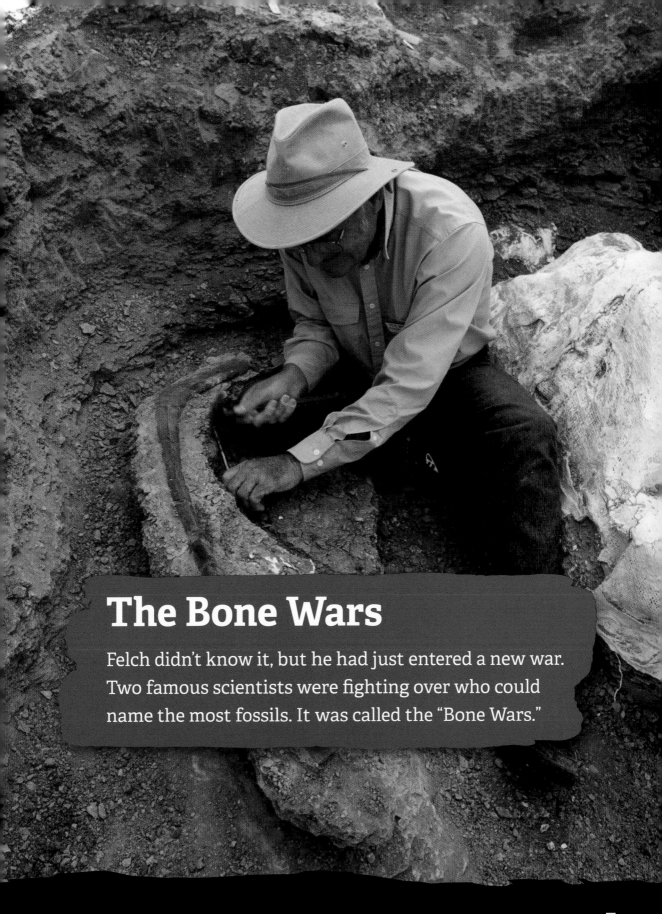

The Bone Wars

Felch didn't know it, but he had just entered a new war. Two famous scientists were fighting over who could name the most fossils. It was called the "Bone Wars."

Felch found those fossils in the winter of 1869–1870. But he had lots of work to do on his new farm. He had to live and work there for five years to make it his own.

In 1877, the local newspaper wrote about the fossils. The article in the *Cañon City Times* talked about the fossils in Felch **Quarry**. That is what they called the rocky place where the bones were found.

A famous scientist read the article. Othniel C. Marsh was a professor at Yale University. He was competing with his old friend Edward Drinker Cope. Both men wanted to name the most fossils.

Professor Marsh sent one of his workers to the farm. Benjamin Franklin Mudge was one of many people who collected fossils for Professor Marsh. He went to Felch Quarry right away. But the fossils still crumbled.

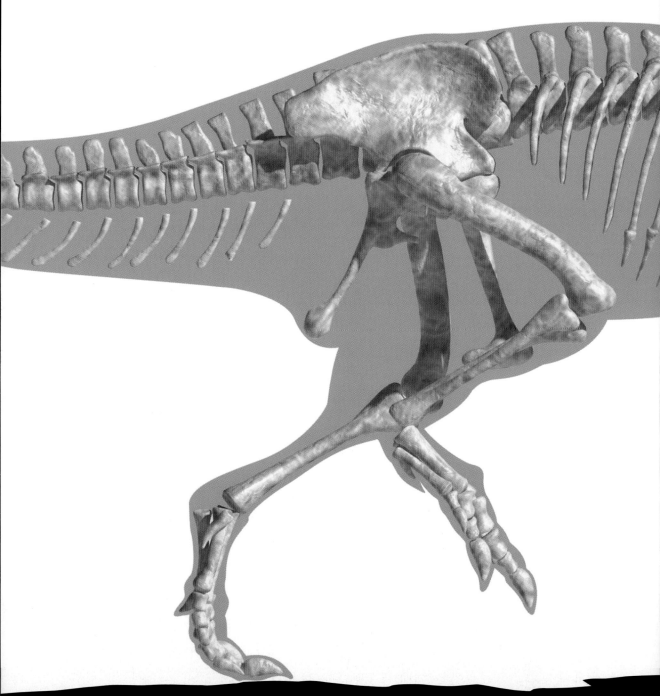

Mudge asked for help. Professor Marsh sent another worker. Samuel W. Williston went out to the quarry. He drew what the bones looked like in the rocks. Then the men placed the crumbled fossils in boxes. They sent the fossils and the drawings to Yale.

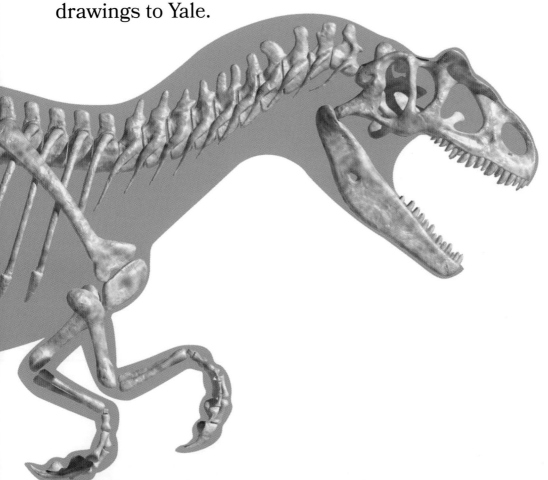

A Fragile Dinosaur

Professor Marsh looked at the drawings and the crumbled fossils. He decided that they were three different dinosaurs. He gave each one a name. One was *Allosaurus fragilis. Allosaurus* means "different lizard." The word *fragilis* means "fragile." This dinosaur had bones with hollow spaces.

MORE NAMES

The Bone Wars continued. More *Allosaurus* bones were found in other places. Professor Marsh gave some of the bones new names. So did his rival. Sometimes they used the same name. Sometimes they used different names. These "bone warriors" gave the same dinosaur nine different names.

Another scientist added two more names. Dr. Ferdinand Hayden was also a fossil hunter. People in another Colorado town gave him a fossil in 1869. He sent it to Dr. Joseph Leidy in Philadelphia. The people thought it was a horse hoof. Dr. Leidy thought it was a tailbone from a dinosaur. He gave it a new name. Then he changed it.

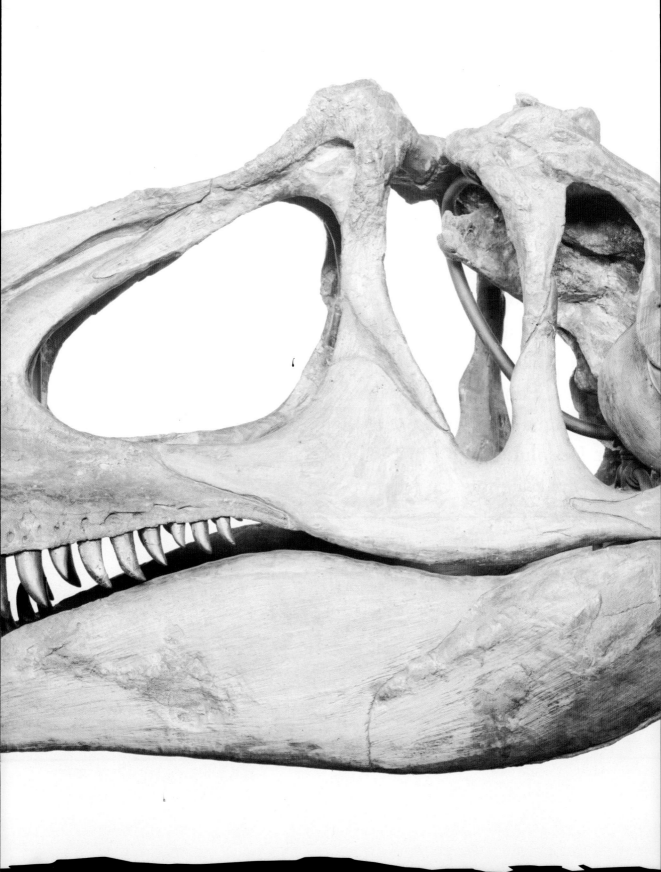

Why did this dinosaur have so many names? Fossils don't come with labels. It takes time to figure out what is in the rocks. Every summer, workers go out to dig up fossils. They study plants and animals buried deep in the rocks. This is the science of paleontology.

Scientists look at the clues. They make notes about how far down they had to dig. They bring the bones back and study them. During the Bone Wars, they were naming fossils as fast as they could. Slow and careful study came later. That is when scientists figured out that this dinosaur had 11 different names!

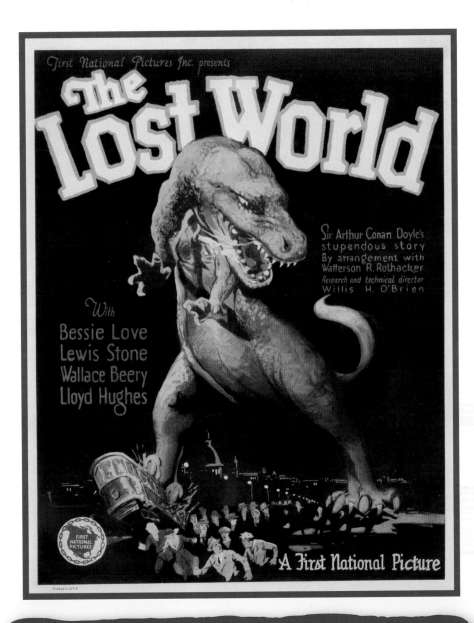

Name #12: Movie Star!

The first full-length dinosaur movie came out in 1925. The movie poster showed a massive dinosaur on the attack. It was an *Allosaurus*! It was the star of the first **Jurassic** dinosaur movie. But you couldn't hear it roar. *The Lost World* was a silent film.

AN APEX PREDATOR

Allosaurus was at the top of the food chain long before it was in the movies. This dinosaur was an **apex** predator. When it was alive, it was on the attack. That became clear after more and more bones were discovered.

In some places, many bones were found together. At first, scientists thought that meant it hunted in packs. But there was not enough evidence to prove it. Just because their bones ended up in the same place didn't mean they hunted together.

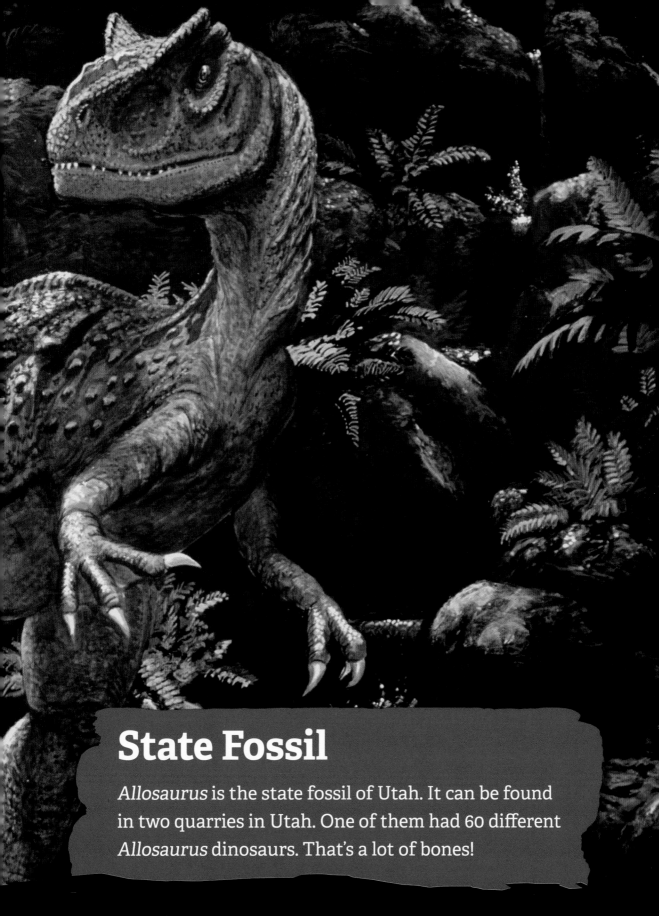

State Fossil

Allosaurus is the state fossil of Utah. It can be found in two quarries in Utah. One of them had 60 different *Allosaurus* dinosaurs. That's a lot of bones!

Allosaurus was a mighty hunter. It had sharp teeth with jagged edges like a saw. These teeth were made for eating meat. This dinosaur was a **carnivore**. Just like a snake, *Allosaurus* could open its jaws very wide. It could gobble big chunks of meat.

Allosaurus was a special kind of meat-eating dinosaur. It was a **theropod**. Theropods had long legs and short arms. They had large heads with big jaws and sharp teeth.

This dinosaur also had horns on its head. These horns were above each eye. They made ridges that looked like eyebrows. Other theropods did not have horns on their heads.

Scientists think this dinosaur ate like a falcon. These birds grasp prey in their claws as they eat. They tear their prey apart bite by bite.

Allosaurus had three fingers on each arm. Each finger had a long, sharp claw. These curved claws could hold prey like a falcon does today.

Falcons can fly fast, but this dinosaur was too big to move quickly. An *Allosaurus* could be 43 feet (13 meters) long from nose to tail. That's longer than some school buses! It could weigh as much as 3,300 pounds (1,497 kilograms).

Allosaurus was certainly taller than a school bus. It could be 16 feet (5 meters) tall. It needed strong legs to carry all of that weight. *Allosaurus* legs ended in feet with three big toes. It also had two tiny toes. One tiny toe pointed backward. The other tiny toe pointed to the side. It was a **dewclaw**. Some dogs and cats today have dewclaws.

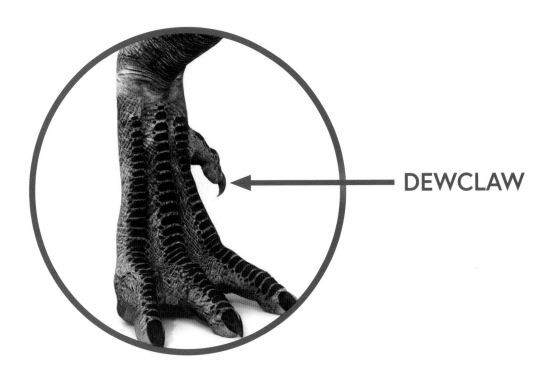

DEWCLAW

How Fast?

Scientists made models to figure out how fast *Allosaurus* could run. They said it may have run as fast as 21 miles (34 kilometers) per hour. That's just a little bit faster than a bus drives in a school zone.

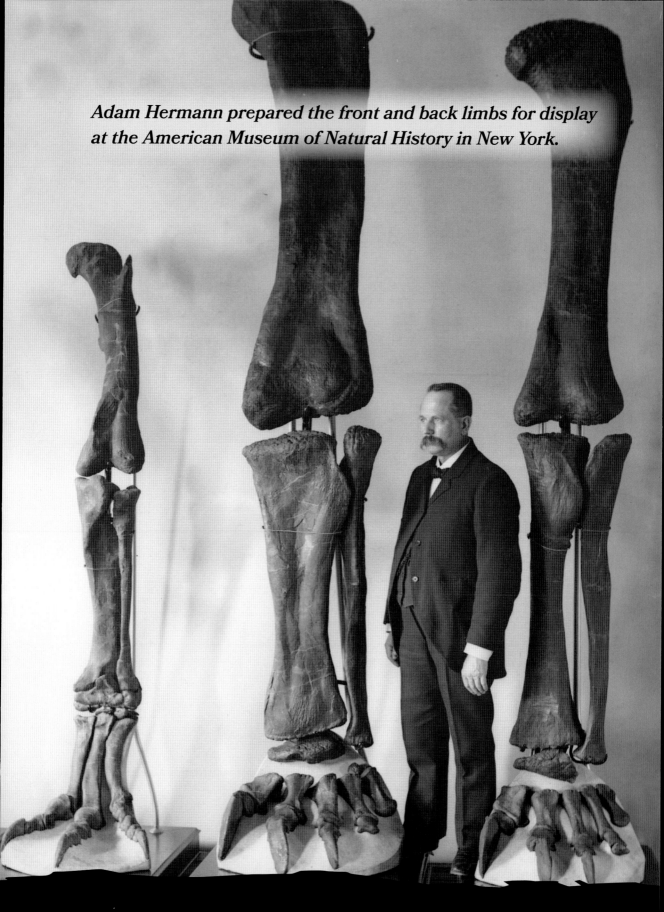

Adam Hermann prepared the front and back limbs for display at the American Museum of Natural History in New York.

Allosaurus couldn't move very fast, but neither could its prey. One of the animals it ate was *Diplodocus*. This plant eater is thought to be the longest dinosaur. One was 90 feet (27 meters) long! Some were even longer.

Allosaurus also ate *Stegosaurus*. This plant eating dinosaur had large plates on its back. These plates were made of bone. They stuck up like spikes. But that didn't stop *Allosaurus* from taking a bite!

The fastest *Diplodocus* could run was nine miles (14 kilometers) per hour. *Stegosaurus* was even slower. It could only run four miles (six kilometers) per hour.

STEGOSAURUS

DIPLODOCUS

EGGS IN A NEST

Scientists have found fossils of *Allosaurus* eggs in nests. They know that all *Allosaurus* hatched from eggs, just like baby chickens do.

An adult *Allosaurus* probably dug a hole in the ground and made a nest. Some theropods laid two eggs at a time. The female *Allosaurus* may have laid 10 to 20 eggs in the nest.

An adult *Allosaurus* was quite large. Sitting on top of the eggs could crush them. Experts think large dinosaurs covered their nests. Dirt or plant matter would have kept the eggs inside the nest warm.

DINOSAUR EGGS

EXTINCT!

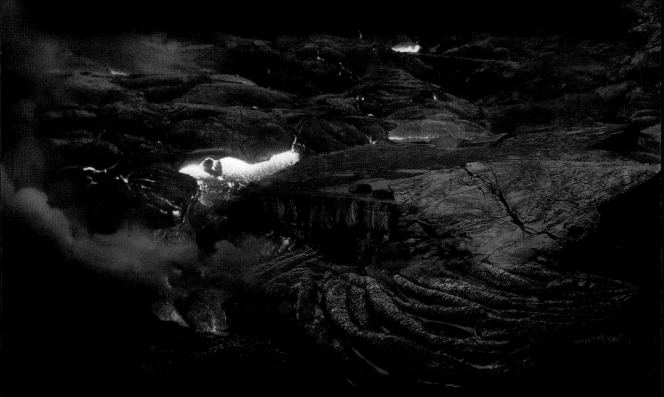

Allosaurus lived long ago during the Jurassic Period. During this time, **pterosaurs** flew in the sky. **Plesiosaurs** swam in the oceans. This tropical world was warm and moist. Forests of conifers and ferns grew. At the end of this time period, many creatures died. Allosaurus was one of them.

In the American West, Allosaurus fossils are what Jurassic fossil hunters find the most. Why did all of the Allosaurus die? Experts think something changed with the food supply. But what caused the food supply to change? Did the climate change? Did an **asteroid** strike Earth? Did a volcano erupt? No one knows.

Don't Be Fooled

Oops! Did you know that *Tyrannosaurus rex* was not a Jurassic dinosaur? Yes, there is a *T. rex* in the *Jurassic Park* movies. But *T. Rex* wasn't alive at that time. *Allosaurus* was the big Jurassic meat eater.

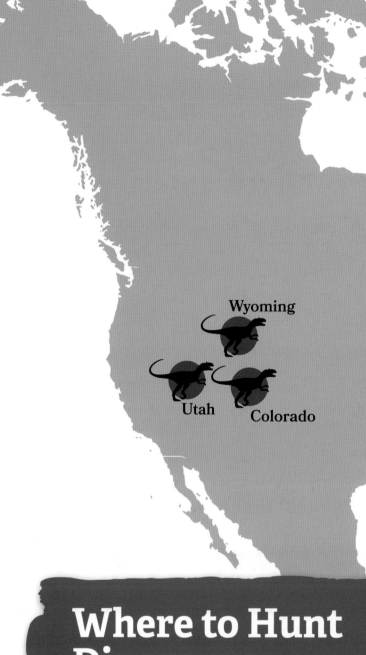

Wyoming

Utah

Colorado

Where to Hunt Dinosaurs

Allosaurus fossils have been found in Colorado, Wyoming, and Utah.

Time Line: *Allosaurus* and You

Do you see yourself on the time line? Look at the far right. You live in the Quaternary Period of the Cenozoic Era. Dinosaurs lived in the era before ours. They roamed the Earth in the Mesozoic Era.

The Mesozoic Era had three time periods. *Allosaurus* lived in the middle time period. They were Jurassic dinosaurs. They lived on Earth about 150 million years ago.

Allosaurus
155–150 million years ago

YOU!

MESOZOIC

CENOZOIC

Triassic	Jurassic	Cretaceous	Tertiary	Quaternary
251–199.6 million years ago	199.6–145.5 million years ago	145.5–65.5 million years ago	65.5–1.81 million years ago	1.81–NOW million years ago

GLOSSARY

apex (AY-peks): at the top; the highest point of something

asteroid (AS-tuh-roid): a rock in space

carnivore (KAHR-nuh-vor): an animal that eats meat

dewclaw (DOO-klaw): a claw or hoof that does not reach the ground

homestead (HOME-sted): a farm and all of its buildings and land

Jurassic (joo-RA-sik): time on Earth from 199.6 to 145.5 million years ago

plesiosaurs (PLEE-see-uh-sors): swimming reptiles that lived in the Jurassic and Cretaceous periods

pterosaurs (TER-uh-sors): flying reptiles that lived in the Jurassic and Cretaceous periods

quarry (KWOR-ee): a place where rock is dug from the ground

theropod (THEER-uh-pahd): a meat-eating, two-legged dinosaur with short arms

INDEX

TEXT-DEPENDENT QUESTIONS

1. Which war did Marshall P. Felch fight in?

2. Why did *Allosaurus* have so many names?

3. Compare an *Allosaurus* and a falcon. How are they alike? How are they different?

4. Describe how *Allosaurus* may have built a nest.

5. Name two dinosaurs *Allosaurus* preyed on.

EXTENSION ACTIVITY

Practice your paleontology skills! Imagine you work at a museum. Create an exhibit about dewclaws. Compare a dog or a cat paw to an *Allosaurus* foot. Use words and images to share information with your museum visitors.

ABOUT THE AUTHOR

Anastasia Suen is the author of more than 300 books for young readers. Her children were both dinosaur fans, so she took them to the Natural History Museum of Los Angeles County and the La Brea Tar Pits often. They called both of these sites the "dinosaur" museum!

www.rourkeeducationalmedia.com

PHOTO CREDITS: Cover and Title Page ©Joe Tucciarone; Pg 4 ©njnightsky; Pg 5 ©François Gohier; Pg 6 ©zrfphoto; Pg 8 ©leonello; Pg 11, 16 ,21 ©American Museum of Natural History Library; Pg 12 ©benedek; Pg 13 ©First National Pictures @ Wiki; Pg 15 ©Chris Butler; Pg 16 ©Charles R. Knight @ wiki; Pg 18 ©MR1805; Pg 19 ©EcoPic, Elenarts, Abscent84; Pg 20 ©JoeLena; Pg 22 ©Gerhard Boeggemann; Pg 23, 29 ©ChrisGorgio; Pg 23 © eamartini; Pg 24 ©Jan Sovak; Pg 25 ©gorosan; Pg 26 ©Jagoush; Pg 28, 29 ©UfimtsevaV; Pg 29 ©ChrisGorgio

Edited by: Kim Thompson
Cover design by: Rhea Magaro-Wallace
Interior design by: Janine Fisher

Library of Congress PCN Data

Allosaurus / Anastasia Suen
 (North American Dinosaurs)
  ISBN 978-1-73161-447-6 (hard cover)
  ISBN 978-1-73161-242-7 (soft cover)
  ISBN 978-1-73161-552-7 (e-Book)
  ISBN 978-1-73161-657-9 (ePub)
Library of Congress Control Number: 2019932147

Rourke Educational Media
Printed in the United States of America,
North Mankato, Minnesota